LUXEMBOURG GARDENS

Information

Candy and toy kiosk

Guard kiosk

Merry-go-round

Playground

Pony rides

Go-carts

Sailboat rental

Music kiosk

Beehive

Public shelter

Restrooms

Statue

Tennis reception

To Paris, where I started to draw.

La La Rose

SATOMI ICHIKAWA

Philomel Books

I am La La Rose, the pink stuffed rabbit. I am the inseparable friend of Clementine.

Today, Grandma takes Clementine and me to the Luxembourg Gardens. Pierre, her brother, comes along.

We go straight to our favorite playground and climb on everything, Clementine and me. We miss nothing.

Then we go on the carousel.
"La La Rose, here we go,"
Clementine says. "Bon voyage!"
I love my Clementine.

When we see the ponies, Clementine begs, "Grandma, please let us ride a pony!"

But Grandma hears the bells ringing. "Later," she says. "It's time for the puppet show now."

They all make a U-turn quickly, except me!
Clementine! I call, but she doesn't hear me.

Now I am all alone. "Caw. Caw. Did you fall out of your nest?" a crow asks me. I am afraid that I did.

A boy picks me up. He cries out, "Look! I found a rabbit!" That's me.

"Let's play!" he says. The boys throw me around and around, and when I land in a trash basket, they shout, "Goal!"

Thank goodness a girl sees me. "What are you doing in here?" she says. "Come with me."
Clementine! I call. Oh, dear . . . Clementine!

Then finally the girl stops. She puts me on the balustrade
and does some exercises.

One-two, one-two.

Where am I? I lean forward to see and I tumble down.
Ouch! Ouch! Ouch!

But a young man with a dog catches me. He throws me
high up in the air. Help!
Will Clementine see me?

Splash! I fall into the water among the sailboats and
the quacking ducks and seagulls. I am in trouble.
But what a good dog—he saves me. Phew!

Then I hear a whistle. A guard arrives. "You are not allowed to let your dog run free in this part of the garden," he says.

"Keep him on a leash," he scolds the young man. I am so wet and dirty—and where is my skirt?

A man with a hat squeezes me gently and puts me in the warm sun next to him. I watch him feeding the sparrows and the pigeons. I am content.

But when the shadows grow long, the man with the hat says, "I have to go home to feed my cats, little rabbit. I wish you good luck." And he leaves me alone. I will never find my Clementine and she will never find me.

A girl with a balloon passes by.
"Has someone lost you, little rabbit?"
she asks me.

I try to nod my head with all my
might. Yes! Yes! Yes!

"I will help you find her," she says.

"Look," says the little girl. She points to a building through the woods. It looks like a mushroom. "Lost people go there," she says.

I am not quite people, but Yes! Yes! Yes! I try to say.

Almost everyone has gone home. Then, through the trees, I see a grandma and little boy and . . . could it be Clementine? "La La Rose!" the girl says. It *is* Clementine!

I found Clementine and she found me. "And
now," Grandma says, "we can take our pony ride!"
Clementine and I are inseparable.

PATRICIA LEE GAUCH, EDITOR

Copyright © 2004 by Satomi Ichikawa

PHILOMEL BOOKS,
a division of Penguin Young Readers Group,
345 Hudson Street, New York, NY 10014.

Published simultaneously in Canada. Manufactured in China by South China Printing Co. Ltd.
Designed by Semadar Megged. Text set in 17.5-point Weiss.
The art was done in watercolor.
Library of Congress Cataloging-in-Publication Data
Ichikawa, Satomi. La La Rose / Satomi Ichikawa. p. cm.
Summary: La La Rose, a young girl's stuffed rabbit, gets lost in Luxembourg Gardens.
[1. Toys—Fiction. 2. Rabbits—Fiction. 3. Lost and found possessions—Fiction. 4. Parks—Fiction.
5. Paris (France)—Fiction. 6. France—Fiction.] I. Title. PZ7.I22555 Lal 2004 [E]—dc21 2002015366
ISBN 0-399-24029-2
1 3 5 7 9 10 8 6 4 2
First Impression